STALKED BY THE SOLDIER

EMMA BRAY

CHAPTER
ONE

Brandon

I'M PARKED at a small table, nursing a black coffee that's already lost its steam. The café buzzes around me, a beehive of clinking cups and idle chatter. I'm just another drone in the mix, but my eyes? They're on the hunt, darting from face to face, looking for...hell, I don't even know. A distraction, maybe. Something to snag my interest.

And then, like flipping a switch, the room brightens a notch. It's not something you see—it's something you feel. My gaze slides across the café and snags on *her*, this burst of color in a sea of drab.

Who is she?

She's got this laugh, you know the kind—sounds like it's bubbling up from a wellspring of pure joy, and damn if it isn't infectious.

She's a few tables over, her head thrown back, auburn hair catching the light as she giggles with the kind of abandon that makes you want to know the joke. Her green eyes sparkle with mischief, and there's this energy about her, like she could dance off into the sunset and leave us all wishing we had an invite.

It's not just her laughter that's got me hooked—it's the whole package. She's the sun, and we're all just orbiting around her, basking in those rays. Every move she makes seems to be in harmony with the universe, and for a second, I forget where I am. I'm not some ex-soldier with too many stories. I'm just Brandon, and I'm completely caught up in this girl— whoever she is.

I lean back, my chair creaking under

the shift of weight. There's something about her, something that lights a fire in my chest. It's been a while since I've felt anything like it, and I'm not about to let it slip away without a fight. This woman has unknowable depths, and I'm itching to dive in, discover every secret smile, every hidden dimple. Hell, I want to know what makes her tick, what throws her into fits of giggles, what stirs that passion I can practically taste from over here.

I sip my cold coffee, my mind already spinning with possibilities.

I hear someone say her name, and my heart skips at beat.

Erica.

It's so perfect, so *her*.

I tap my fingers on the edge of the table, trying not to make it too obvious that I'm now fully tuned into Erica's frequency. It's like there's a spotlight just on her, and damn if my heart isn't doing this funny little skip every time she throws her head back to laugh. My gaze drinks in her every move, lapping up the way she brushes her hair behind an ear or tucks a loose strand back into the wild cascade.

"Take it easy, soldier," I mutter under my breath, trying to remind myself to keep it cool. But who am I kidding? Cool flew out the window the moment those green eyes sparkled with all the secrets of the universe.

I lean slightly to the left, seeking a clearer view as she animatedly gestures to accentuate a story she must be telling. The simple act of lifting her coffee cup to those lips—lips that are surely as soft and inviting as they look—sends my pulse racing like I'm back on a mission, adrenaline pumping through my veins.

"Focus, Brandon," I scold myself. But it's useless. I'm locked in, utterly captivated by the living art piece that is *her*. She moves like she's part of some divine choreography, every tilt of the head and flutter of lashes seeming to sync perfectly with the hum of life around us.

The clink of ceramic on wood snaps me out of my reverie—Erica's setting down her cup, and I'm setting a course to know her. What's behind those emerald eyes? Is her laugh always this full, like a melody that's found its perfect rhythm in the chaos of the world?

To others, she might just be another face in the crowd, but not to me. She's a puzzle I'm itching to solve, a story I want to read from cover to cover, savoring every damn word.

I stand, my chair scraping quietly against the floor. It's time for some intel—a deep dive into the enigma wrapped in that radiant smile. My soldier instincts kick into high gear, scanning for the best exit. No need to alert her to my interest...not yet.

Back in my apartment, the glow of the computer screen cuts through the dimness. I crack my knuckles—it's go time. The keys click-clack under my fingers, each stroke a step closer to unraveling the mystery of Erica. I type her name into the search bar, feeling like a modern-day knight on a quest, minus the shining armor.

"Let's see what you're all about," I say, half expecting the internet to whisper back secrets only it knows. Thumbnails of her art pop up, splashes of color that scream passion and depth. My gut tightens with anticipation. Each piece is a clue, a fragment of her fervent soul.

I click through gallery after gallery, absorbing the vibrant life she pours into every brushstroke. This woman isn't just living. She's alive in a way that sets my blood on fire.

I lean in, the glow of the screen turning my focus into something laser-sharp. Erica's art is a rabbit hole, and damn if I'm not tumbling down it headfirst. Each painting, each sculpture, it's like she's baring her soul to the world, and I can't get enough. My fingers fly across the keyboard, hungry for more—her favorite books, interviews, any breadcrumb that leads me closer to understanding who Erica Rose really is.

"Jane Austen and Kurt Vonnegut?" I whistle low, impressed. Girl's got taste. Classic romance with a side of satirical sci-fi. It paints a picture in my mind of her curled up on a couch, losing herself in 'Pride and Prejudice' or 'Slaughterhouse-

Five.' Damn, wouldn't I love to be a fly on that wall?

"Ah, there's the gold," I murmur as I find a blog post she wrote about living life to the fullest. She talks about seizing the day, finding inspiration in the mundane, and always chasing the next adventure. Her words light a fire in me, and I feel this pull, like she's already challenging me to step up my own game.

But then, the well runs dry. Click after click leads to dead-ends, private profiles, and frustratingly brief bios. "Come on, give me something to work with here," I grumble, scouring page after forgotten page of search results. It shouldn't be this hard to find out about someone so vibrant, should it? The irony isn't lost on me—a trained soldier stumped by the lack of intel on a civilian.

"Erica, you're killing me," I say to the empty room, scratching at my jaw where stubble is starting to form. With every dead link, my curiosity morphs into something raw, an itch I desperately need to scratch. But the digital paper trail has gone cold, and I'm left hanging, wondering what makes her tick, what her laugh sounds like up close, how her skin feels under my—

"Focus, Brandon." I shake my head, clearing the X-rated thoughts. Can't let the frustration mess with my head. There's got to be another way to crack this code, to find the key to Erica's enigma. And I'll be damned if I don't find it.

I hit refresh for what feels like the hundredth time, my eyes glued to the glow of the computer screen. There's a stubborn part of me that refuses to give up, and it's running on pure, undiluted hope. Suddenly, the pixels rearrange themselves into something promising—a link I haven't seen before, shining like a beacon in the digital darkness.

"Hello, what's this?" I mutter, clicking through, and there it is—jackpot. It's a social media profile, not locked down by privacy settings, and it's all Erica. My heart kicks up a notch as I scroll through her timeline, taking in every post, every shared quote, every piece of her that's been laid out online for the world to see.

Each image is a window straight into

her life, and damn, she's even more extraordinary than I realized. Pictures of her paintings, vibrant and full of life, splashes of color that tell stories I'm desperate to hear her speak out loud. There are snapshots of her at art shows, her smile as wide as the canvas she stands beside, pride written all over her face.

And then I find it—the connection that zaps through me like a live wire. A photo of her holding a dog-eared copy of "The Great Gatsby," the caption quoting Fitzgerald right off the page I know by heart. That book's been my companion through countless lonely nights, and seeing it in her hands—it's like finding a piece of myself in her grip.

A grin spreads across my face. Our shared passions unspool before me—a love for art that speaks, books that feel like old friends, and a zest for life that refuses to be caged. The excitement builds in my chest, a heady mix of adrenaline and something sweeter, warmer. It's anticipation, pure and simple, the kind that makes you want to run headlong into the unknown because you just know it's going to be incredible.

And then I stumble across a picture of her on the beach.

In a little white bikini.

Hot damn.

My eyes trail over her flawless skin, long legs, tiny waist, hair flowing down her back, ass perky and round. She's peeking back at the camera over her shoulder. Cute and flirty and playful.

My cock is instantly hard and leaking.

I hesitate only a moment before I unzip my pants and pull it out.

My hand wraps tightly around my length, the image of Erica in that little white bikini burned into my retinas. I pump myself slowly, savoring the raw, primal hunger that settles deep in my gut.

She's a vision—a wet dream come to life, her curves and the playful glint in her eyes weaving an intoxicating spell. My thumb rubs over the sensitive head of my cock, sending jolts of pleasure skittering along my spine. I'm consumed by the image of her in that bikini, all sunshine and bare skin and endless legs.

"Fuck," I groan, leaning back in my chair and letting my head fall back. The room is silent but for the harsh sound of my breathing echoing off the bare walls. My free hand roams over my abdomen, fingers tracing the rigid muscles there. Each heavy breath makes them flex under my touch.

The more I stroke myself, the more vividly I can picture her—those expressive green eyes staring straight into mine as she gyrates on top of me, those full lips parted in a sigh of pleasure. My strokes speed up at the thought, quick and rough and frantic.

I imagine her soft hands replacing mine, her fingers wrapped around me as she works me to a fever pitch. The fantasy is so potent, I can almost feel her warm breath against my neck and hear her whispered encouragements in my ear.

"Fuck Erica..." I mutter to myself, picturing her beneath me—those long legs wrapped around my waist as I drive into her, again and again.

I'm close now—so fucking close—and all I can think of is Erica

—her laughter, her passion, her fiery spirit. The image of her in that bikini, the way she'd look at me with those emerald eyes, the sounds she'd make as I slid inside her...

"God damn," I pant, my hand moving faster and faster. The pleasure is wild, untamed, coursing through my veins like molten lava. The need to see her, touch her, claim her crashes into me like a tidal wave, and I surrender to it fully.

Her name is a prayer on my lips as I come, shooting thick ropes of cum onto my hand and the hardwood floor beneath me. My orgasm is so intense it blurs my vision, and all I can see is the ghost of her body pressed against mine.

"Fuck." The word slips out ragged and raw as I slump back in my chair, my chest heaving wildly.

I'm spent. Exhausted. But there's no satisfaction in this release—not when it's a phantom version of Erica that's driving me wild.

I clean myself up quickly before zipping my pants again and refocusing on the screen.

I run a hand through my hair as I scroll through more of her photos—a spontaneous trip to Italy here, an intimate moment with a paintbrush there—each one adding color to the canvas of who she is.

She's got this profound love for life that's infectious even through these digital fragments. She isn't just an artist. She is art, captivating and untamed.

I let out a sigh, longing clawing at my insides. I want this woman. Not just in my bed, but in my life. I want to explore the depths of her mind, to be captivated by her creativity, to be there when she's vulnerable.

That thought scares the hell out of me, but it's a fear I'm willing to face. I've fought through war zones, stood toe-to-toe with death on more than one occasion, but this? This feels like the most important battle I've ever faced.

The need to see her in person grows stronger with every heartbeat. The screen suddenly feels like a barrier rather than a window into her world.

It's not enough.

I *need* her.

CHAPTER
TWO

Erica

THE STEAM from my latte whispers secrets just before I send it flying across the table. "Shit!" It's like slow motion, hot liquid spreading a map of chaos over the white surface, seeping toward innocent bystanders in the form of scones and smartphones.

"Here, let me help with that." The voice is deep, calm amidst my personal espresso hurricane. I look up, and holy fuck. Who is this guy? He's all muscled and buff and he has these piercing blue eyes that are locked onto mine as if he's assessing a battlefield. Is he military? He *looks* military. But instead of a soldier's command, he offers a white napkin, his movements deft, sure.

"Thanks," I murmur, cheeks blazing hotter than the spilled drink. My heart thuds, not from the embarrassment, but from the closeness of him—this guy who looks like he could carry the weight of the world on his shoulders without breaking a sweat. His hands, large and capable, work alongside mine to blot the coffee flood, his fingers brushing against mine with subtle intention.

"Looks like your coffee tried to make a break for it, huh?" he quips, a corner of his mouth lifting in a half-smile that ignites something reckless inside me. His touch is light, careful, not missing a beat or a drop of the rogue brew.

"Damn, you've got a reflex like a cat," I say, half-laughing despite the disaster in front of me. His quick hands are already sweeping up the last of my latte from the table, his grin easy and infectious.

"Only when it comes to saving beautiful women from the tyranny of rogue coffee," he responds, the teasing note in his voice drawing a reluctant smile from my lips.

I can't help but feel a rush of warmth at his words—not just from the compliment, but also from his willingness to dive into the fray with me. "I'm usually not this clumsy, I swear."

"Don't worry about it," he says, tossing the soaked napkins onto the growing pile. "It gives character to the place. Plus, now we have an epic tale of bravery and sacrifice to tell our grandkids."

His joke has me barking out a laugh, the sound sharp and sudden in the quiet café. "Our grandkids? You move fast considering I don't even know your name."

"Brandon," he gives me a full smile. "And you are?"

"Erica," I tell him.

Brandon.

"And I only move this fast when I see something—or someone—I like." His eyes twinkle with mirth, and there's an edge of sincerity beneath his playful words that sends a tingle through me.

"Is that so?" I tilt my head, intrigued by the twist in our conversation. "Well, thank you for the save...again."

"Anytime," he says, and the simple word carries a promise that knots my stomach with a mix of nerves and excitement. The mess is all but forgotten as we stand there, the air between us charged with something new, something with potential.

"Guess I owe you one now," I add, biting my lip as I consider him. There's a depth to Brandon I hadn't noticed before, a gentleness that contradicts his rugged exterior.

"Consider it a freebie," he counters, "but if you insist on repaying me, I wouldn't say no to grabbing dinner with you."

The forwardness of his invitation catches me off guard, but the eager flutter in my chest tells me I'm not opposed to the idea.

Not at all.

I slide into the booth, the warmth of the dimly lit restaurant wrapping around us like a cozy blanket. A soft melody plays in the background, just loud enough to soothe without drowning out conversation. The table is set with candles flickering in the draft, their dance reflecting in Brandon's eyes as he watches me across the table.

"Is it just me or did we step into someone's living room?" I quip, glancing around at the plush cushions and intimate spaces between tables.

"Only if your living room serves a five-star beef wellington," he retorts, humor sparkling in his gaze.

Our laughter mingles and fades as a waiter sets down plates of steaming food, the aromas mingling and rising to greet our senses. Brandon's steak is cooked to perfection, its savory scent making my mouth water. My pasta, a tangle of freshly made noodles and rich sauce, beckons with a promise of comfort.

"This looks amazing," I say, twirling my fork through the pasta.

"Yes, it does," he agrees, but he's not even looking at his steak as he cuts it.

He's looking at *me*.

My heart does this funny flip in my chest.

Dinner with Brandon isn't just about the food, although that's good too. It's the conversation, laced with wit, sprinkled with shared interests and peppered with deep, sincere confessions. He talks about his time in the military with a candor that surprises me. Despite the danger and hardships he faced, he speaks of those years with a sense of pride and purpose.

"And what about you, Erica? Tell me about your art," he asks, looking at me with genuine interest. His elbows are propped up on the table, his chin resting on his clasped hands as though my words are the most important thing in the world to him.

I tell him about my passion for painting, how I can lose myself for hours in colors and textures. I talk about how each piece feels like giving away a part of my soul. It's intense, but it's also liberating. As I speak, Brandon's gaze never wavers from mine. He absorbs every word, every inflection, every emotion that colors my voice.

I've never felt so...watched. In a good way.

Laughter punctuates our dinner as we share stories—some funny, some painful. And when we broach more serious topics —war for him and artistic struggle for me —there is an understanding there that is both comforting and thrilling.

"Who knew," he muses after we've finished our meal, leaning back in his chair and regarding me thoughtfully. "A soldier and an artist finding common ground."

"Why not?" I challenge, my tone matching his playful one. "Art is about expression, about conveying a message or a feeling. Isn't that what you do in your field? You fight for a cause, for a feeling of security and peace."

Brandon nods, the flickering candle-light casting an appealing shadow across his chiseled features. "Never thought of it that way, but you're right. It's about passion, isn't it? Both our fields require a certain...fire."

I feel that fire now as he reaches across the table, taking my hand in his. There's an intimacy in this small gesture that makes my breath hitch. "You certainly have that passion, Erica. It's one of the things I find most attractive about you."

His words stun me into silence. I've never been so bold, so forward with someone I just met. But there's something about Brandon that makes me want to explore more, unearth the layers beneath his hardened exterior.

"Do you want to continue this somewhere else?" He queries, breaking the comfortable silence between us.

"Like where?" I ask, fighting the urge to squeeze his hand just a little tighter.

"Let's walk," he suggests, standing up and extending his other hand to help me out of the booth.

Hand in hand, we exit the cozy restaurant and step out into the crisp night air. The city is alive with lights and sounds, but all I can focus on is the warmth of Brandon's hand wrapped around mine.

We walk aimlessly for a while, our conversation ebbing and flowing as naturally as if we'd known each other forever. We talk about everything and nothing at all. Shared likes and dislikes weave an invisible thread between us, strengthening the connection we had ignited in the café.

As we wander past a quaint bookstore tucked into a corner of the street, Brandon pulls me towards it. "You like books, right?" he asks, his eyes gleaming with a mischievous spark.

"I do," I affirm, my heart pounding in anticipation of what he might have planned.

Inside, the soothing scent of old books wafts to meet us. The warm glow of soft yellow lights casts long shadows on the wooden shelves filled to the brim with books of every shape, size, and genre. It's like stepping into another world—a quiet, cozy world where time seems to slow down and every moment is imbued with a sense of magic and wonder.

We browse through the shelves

together, pointing out favorite novels and authors. But when Brandon picks up a copy of 'Pride and Prejudice', my favorite classic novel, my heart swells with unexpected delight.

"Let's sit," he says, guiding me towards a pair of plush armchairs nestled in a quiet corner of the bookstore. As we sink into the comfortable seats, he opens the book and begins reading aloud. His voice is deep and soothing—a comforting balm that perfectly complements the familiar words of Jane Austen's timeless love story.

Every now and then, our eyes meet above the pages. There's a wordless exchange that happens in those moments—an intimate understanding that transcends the awkwardness typical of new relationships. It's as if we are getting lost in our own romantic tale, one that intertwines seamlessly with Elizabeth Bennet and Mr. Darcy's courtship.

Hours seem to pass as seconds as we share stories and quotes from other beloved books. I'd never thought a date in a bookstore could be so damn sexy. But everything about tonight, about Brandon, is wildly unexpected and beautiful.

Eventually, we leave the bookstore and resume our meandering walk. The city sleeps around us, but we're wide awake, fueled by our electrifying connection and the magic of the night. His hand in mine sends waves of anticipation coursing through me. Each casual touch sparks something deep within me.

Before I realize it, we're standing in front of my apartment building. My heart flutters with a mix of nervousness and excitement as Brandon turns to face me. His intense gaze takes my breath away.

"I had a fantastic time tonight, Erica," he says, his voice low and sincere. "Could I see you again?"

The question hangs heavy in the cool night air between us. My heart hammers in my chest as I meet his eyes.

"I'd like that," I reply softly. My words seem to ignite something in him. His piercing blue eyes are ablaze with emotion that mirrors my own.

It feels like something big is happening here, something bigger than a spilled cup of coffee or an accidental meeting at a café. It's a beginning, a start of something new and thrilling—something that promises adventures, shared conversations, intertwined hands, limbs.

My cheeks flush at the turn my thoughts just took.

"Goodnight Erica," he whispers against my ear before pressing his warm lips on my cheek—a sweet promise for another day.

As I climb up to my apartment, I can't help but replay every moment of our date – from the cozy restaurant to browsing the bookstore and finally this innocent yet intimate goodnight kiss on the cheek.

Brandon. The soldier who I suddenly feel like I've known forever.

CHAPTER
THREE

Brandon

I SLIP my hand into Erica's as we wander through the maze of canvases and sculptures, her fingers a perfect fit with mine. Her laugh is a melody that hooks deep in my chest, more captivating than any piece of art we've passed today.

"Look at this one," she says, pulling me toward an abstract splash of colors that I can't make heads or tails of. But the way her eyes light up, like she's just stumbled upon buried treasure, makes me want to see the world through her lens.

"Explain it to me," I say, because half the fun is listening to her talk, seeing her get all fired up about brush strokes and symbolism.

She tilts her head, studying the chaos on the canvas before diving into an explanation about emotion and expression. I catch maybe one word in three, but her passion—it's fucking infectious.

"Brandon, are you even listening?" Erica nudges me with a teasing smile, and I have to grin back.

"Every word," I lie.

"Sure," she chuckles, giving me a playful shove. It's our thing—her knowing I'm full of it but loving me anyway. Or so I hope.

"Come on, let's grab some air," I suggest, leading her out of the gallery. The city park waits outside, drenched in sunset hues, its paths winding like ribbons through verdant lawns.

We take a leisurely stroll, her head occasionally resting against my shoulder. I memorize these moments, storing them as if they're precious metals, because who knows how long before I'm shipped off again.

"Are you hungry?" Erica asks, breaking the comfortable silence.

"Starving, but first, I've got a surprise." I can't help the excitement bubbling in my voice as I pull two tickets from my pocket. "Tonight, your favorite band is playing downtown."

Her mouth drops open, and I swear her eyes are brighter than the stars beginning to prick the evening sky. "Brandon! How?"

"Let's just say I have my ways," I wink, and her laughter fills the space between us.

Fast forward, and there we are, right in the heart of the concert frenzy. The thumping bass echoes in my ribcage, somehow in sync with my heartbeat. Erica's dancing beside me, her body a mesmerizing rhythm I'm itching to match.

"Come on, soldier, show me what you've got!" she shouts over the music, grinning wide and wicked.

And damn if I don't rise to the challenge. Our bodies move together, getting lost in the beats, the lyrics, the sheer energy of the crowd around us. She sings along, slightly off-key but totally unashamed, and it's the hottest thing ever.

"Kiss me, Brandon!" she yells, and it's not a request—it's a command. One I'm all too happy to obey.

Our lips crash together, and it's like fireworks and lightning strikes all at once. It's messy and desperate and perfect, and I pour everything I am into that kiss. We're not just dancing now. We're creating something new, something wild.

"Erica," I murmur against her lips, and her name is a prayer, a promise, a plea.

"More," she breathes out, and we're kissing again, hands roaming, hearts racing.

The band plays on, but for us, they might as well be a million miles away. We're in our own world now—a world where every note is a caress, every drum-beat a heartbeat, and the night is ours for the taking.

I feel my cock growing hard, and it takes everything in me not to throw her onto the floor and hump her like a rabid dog in front of everyone.

I resist—but just barely.

———

I'm a bundle of nerves, sitting across from Erica in this dimly lit café that's become our haven away from the world. My hands are fidgety on the table, and there's this knot in my stomach that's been tightening all evening. It's time, I decide. Time to let her in on the part of me that's still marching in formation, even when I'm out of uniform.

I need her to know the truth. I don't want any secrets from her. She needs to know the type of man that I really am.

"Erica," I start, voice barely above a whisper, "I gave you a watered down version of my life as a soldier before, but now I need to tell you the truth about my time in the service." She leans forward, green eyes locked onto mine, full of warmth and concern.

It's now or never.

As words tumble out—about brotherhood, the weight of a rifle, the taste of dust—I watch her face. She's a statue of compassion, absorbing every word like it's sacred. I tell her about the days that were too hot, the nights that were too long, the friends that became family. She reaches across the table, her touch grounding me when memories threaten to sweep me away.

"Brandon, thank you for sharing this with me," she says, squeezing my hand. "You're not alone anymore, okay?"

"Okay," I echo, and it feels like a goddamn revelation. My sweet, beautiful girl. She's heard it all. The dirty details, all the nitty gritty, and she didn't run for the hills.

She really is perfect.

———

Fast forward to that golden hour when the sun starts playing coy, dipping below the horizon. We're perched on a quiet hilltop, the city sprawling beneath us like a kingdom of lights. I pull Erica close, her body fitting against mine like she's always belonged there.

"Look at that view," she murmurs, but I can't take my eyes off her. The last rays of sunlight make her hair shine like molten copper, and I'm struck by an urge so fierce it almost takes my breath away.

Every night, I'm haunted by fantasies of her—her skin, her sounds, her taste. It's a hunger that gnaws at me, relentless and raw. But I keep it caged because I want our first time to be more than just physical release. I want it to be a testament to what she means to me.

I try to steer my thoughts to safer waters. She smiles up at me, eyes reflecting the twilight and the stars beginning to peek through.

"Tell me your dreams," she insists, her fingers tracing patterns on my arm that send shivers down my spine.

"This," I confess, voice thick with emotion. "I dream of this."

She blinks up at me innocently, her lips parting on a gasp. And I can't help it. I have to lean down and kiss her.

My cock is leaking like a sieve in my

pants. It's been hell on it staying hard all damn day. But I'd suffer through anything for her.

We make out like a couple of high school kids, and I sense that she would let me take it furhter.

I'm tempted. God, how I'm tempted.

But I can't. I know I'll lose control if I do. My obsession with her is too potent.

So, I just hold her tighter as darkness wraps around us.

This is it, the real deal. And I'm scared as hell of losing it, especially with deployment looming over me like a storm cloud. But right here, right now, with Erica in my arms, I let myself believe in something good on the horizon. Something worth fighting for.

CHAPTER
FOUR

Brandon

"DOUBLE SHOT OF ESPRESSO, please, and a vanilla latte for the lady," I tell the barista, my voice a steady rhythm amidst the clinking of cups and the hiss of the steam wand at the café. It's our regular spot, a cozy corner where Erica's laughter often mingles with the scent of roasted beans. I glance back at her, my eyes tracing the curve of her smile, the way her hair tumbles like autumn leaves over her shoulders. She's got this glow, you know?

Like she carries her own personal sunrise wherever she goes.

As I wait for our order, that's when *he* walks in.

Lucas.

I recognize him from Erica's social media pages.

The childhood buddy turned suave charmer with a jawline sharp enough to cut glass. I have to admit that even though I know nothing ever happened between Erica and him, hearing about how close she was with this childhood friend made me all sorts of jealous.

I watch him. He's all casual confidence, strolling through life like it owes him one. And suddenly, he's making a beeline for Erica's table, unaware I'm even in the picture, much less in her life.

My gut tightens, a coil of snakes awakened by the intrusion. I can't hear their words from here, but I see the surprise flicker across Erica's face, a storm of emotions passing through those expressive green eyes. Confusion, nostalgia—damn, it's like watching a silent movie, and I'm not enjoying the show.

"Here you go, sir," the barista hands me the coffees, her cheerfulness lost on me. "Thanks," I mutter, but my focus is locked on the tableau unfolding across the room.

Lucas leans in, all smiles and reminiscence. Erica's polite, yeah, but there's a distance there, a wall she's put up quicker than a New York minute. Still, it's like a punch to the chest, watching them. My jaw clenches so hard I could chew nails for breakfast.

My feet itch to stalk over there, but I let the scene play out. Erica's handling it, isn't she? Doesn't need me swooping in like some overprotective hawk. But damn, my fists are balled up tight, knuckles itching for something to hit.

"Sir, your coffees are getting cold," the barista gives me a nudge, snapping me back to the present. Right, the coffees. I grab the tray, the heat from the cups barely registering as I continue to watch my girl.

I can't take it anymore. My boots pound the café floor like a drumbeat of war as I march toward their table. Erica's eyes widen, but it's Lucas who gets my glare, the kind that's made grown men rethink their life choices.

"Erica," I say, my voice a low growl, "we need to talk."

She blinks at me, her mouth parting in surprise. Lucas, the smooth operator, tries to slide back into the conversation with a chuckle that grates on every last nerve I have. But I'm done playing nice.

I don't wait for her response. I gently take her arm and pull her outside with me.

"Brandon?" Her voice is a mix of confusion and concern, but there's a tremor there that tells me she feels the gravity of this moment too.

We burst out of the café, the cool air slapping some sense into me—but not enough to douse the fire raging inside. She's right behind me, her steps quick and light, the opposite of the heavy thud of my heart.

"Brandon?" Erica's voice is a tentative quesiton.

"Couldn't sit there one more second

watching him cozy up to you," I admit, my words tumbling out raw and jagged.

"Jealous much?" There's a teasing lilt to her words, but her eyes are searching mine, looking for the truth beneath the bravado.

"Damn right I am," I say, owning it, laying it all out there. "I've never wanted anyone the way I want you, Erica."

Her breath hitches, and I know I've struck a chord. The air between us crackles with something fierce, something that feels a lot like destiny. And I'd fight wars to keep it, keep her.

I grab Erica's shoulders, my fingers digging in just a bit too hard. The streetlight casts an amber glow on her face, painting her in shades of gold and shadow. "Look at me, Erica," I demand, my voice barely above a whisper but heavy with emotion.

She tilts her chin up, her green eyes wide and luminous. They're like twin beacons, pulling me into their depths, drowning me in feelings I've been trying to keep caged.

"Lucas doesn't matter," I begin, my

words coming fast. "He's the past. You and me...we're right here, right now. And damn it, I'm scared shitless."

"Brandon..." she starts, but I shake my head, cutting her off.

"No, let me finish. I have to say this." I take a deep breath, feeling like I'm at the edge of a cliff, ready to dive into the unknown. "I am so fucking in love with you that it terrifies me. Every time I think about you walking away from me, or him—or anyone—sneaking back into your life, it's like someone's squeezing my heart in a vise."

Her lips part, and she leans into me just a fraction, like she's drawn by the intensity pouring out of me.

"Every mission I've been on, every order I've followed—it's all clear-cut, black and white. But this—us—it's a mess of colors, and yet, I've never been more certain about anything. I want you, Erica. All of you. Your laughter, your art, your passion, your fears. I'll take it all."

"Brandon, I—" She falters, and I can see the conflict playing out across her beautiful features.

"Say it," I urge, desperate for her to understand. "Tell me what you're thinking."

"I'm scared too," she whispers, her voice trembling. "Your job, your duty...they could take you away from me. How do we build a life around that uncertainty?"

My stomach falls because fuck she's right. This is what I've been afraid of too, isn't it? It's why I haven't allowed myself to claim her the way I want to yet.

Because deep down I know it's selfish. It's selfish of me to take her knowing what could happen with my work.

Her hand comes up to touch my cheek, her touch light as a feather but strong enough to send shock waves through my entire body.

She doesn't speak, and I don't speak. Hell, I can't speak. All I can do is swallow and try not to cry as I watch her walk away.

———

I try. In my defense, I try. I really do.

But I can't fucking stay away from her. She's gotten under my skin, and it's not even an hour before I'm charging down the street to her apartment.

I pound on the door like I'm the motherfucking police. It opens, and there she is—Erica, standing in the dimly lit hallway looking like a vision that's just too good to be true. Her eyes lock with mine, green pools of uncertainty and longing that I'm desperate to dive into.

"What are you doing here?" she breathes out, her voice a melody that hits all the right notes inside me.

"I can't, Erica. I just can't." My words are rough around the edges, a reflection of the storm of emotions churning inside me.

She step back to allow me inside. My body brushes against hers, and the closeness sends a jolt through my body. The door clicks shut, and it's just us.

She looks down and wrings her hands together, a telltale sign that she's nervous.

I plow right in. "Erica, I get it, I do. But damn it, I can't lose you over maybes and what-ifs." My heart pounds against my ribcage, fighting for release.

"Neither can I," she confesses, stepping closer. "But Brandon, what if—"

"Shh." I close the distance between us in two strides, my hands finding her waist. "No more what-ifs."

She looks up at me, her lips parting slightly, and I can't hold back any longer. I pull her to me, crashing my lips onto hers with an urgency that leaves no room for doubt. This kiss—it's a declaration, a battle cry, a promise of everything I am and ever will be.

Her arms wind around my neck, pulling me down into her gravity. Our bodies press close, every curve of her fitting into me like she's made for this moment, for *me*. The room is alive with the sound of our breaths mingling, the hum of desire so thick I could reach out and touch it.

"Erica," I groan against her mouth, and she responds with a fervor that lights me up from the inside.

"Brandon," she whispers back, and that's all it takes to seal the deal—to know that whatever comes next, we're in it together, come hell or high water.

As we break for air, our foreheads rest against each other, and I swear I can feel the beat of her heart syncing with mine, a silent vow that speaks louder than words ever could.

The world narrows to Erica and me, our footsteps a clumsy dance as we weave toward the bedroom. My fingers trace the outline of her spine, slipping beneath the fabric of her shirt, hungry for the warmth of her skin. She matches my urgency, tugging at the hem of my tee, pulling it over my head with a swift, almost frenzied motion.

"Brandon," she breathes out, her voice laced with need. Her hands roam over my chest, nails grazing lightly, sending shivers down my spine that have nothing to do with the cool air of the room.

"God, Erica," I rasp, fumbling with the button on her jeans, desperate to rid her of any barrier that keeps her from me. Our clothes shed like leaves in fall, discarded without care.

Our bodies collide—a perfect storm of want and will—crashing onto the mattress. Her hair fans out around her on the pillow, a fiery halo that ignites some-thing primal in me. I lower my lips to hers, tasting the sweet promise of forever mixed with the salt of anticipation.

I take a moment to just admire how beautiful her naked body is. My cock is leaking, and I give myself a rough stroke as I stare down at her slack-jawed.

"Fucking beautiful," I breathe out, my voice vibrating with raw lust. Her cheeks blush a deep shade of red at the compli-ment but she doesn't turn away, instead boldly meeting my gaze.

My fingers trail down her torso to the wetness pooling between her legs. She shivers as I slip two fingers inside, her hips arching off the bed with a sigh that sounds like heaven.

"Oh god, Brandon," she mumbles, her voice breathy and desperate. Her hands grab onto my arms, nails digging into my skin just enough that it has me gritting my teeth.

"Tell me this is what you want Erica," I demand, needing to hear her confirmation just as much as I need air. The last thing I want is her regretting this in the morning.

"Yes...I want this Brandon...I want you," she gasps out. It's all the encouragement I need.

My hard cock finds her entrance, and we both moan at the sensation of being so intimately connected. I thrust slowly at first, giving Erica time to adjust to me—holy fuck, is she a virgin? The knowledge that I'm going to be the only man inside of her does something insane to me.

My cock gets even harder, and I can't sit still any longer.

Must move.

Must make her mine.

Mine, mine, mine!

"Fuck...Erica..." I grumble into the crook of her neck, my pace quickening with every stroke.

She wraps her legs around me tighter, pulling me deeper into her until our bodies are flush against each other, leaving no space for anything else.

"I-I'm going to..." she stammers out just as I feel her walls clamp down on me. Her orgasm sends me over the edge.

"Erica," I groan, feeling her tighten around me, her body gripping mine in a vice of passion. I capture her lips again, swallowing her cries as I continue to thrust inside her.

"More," she whispers, her fingers digging into my shoulders. I give her what she asks for, what I need too—the unbridled release, the raw intensity of two souls entwined.

Another climax rips through her, a tidal wave that crashes into me, dragging me under until I'm lost in the depths of her. My own release follows, a surge of heat that brands her name onto every cell of my being.

"Erica," I pant, spent, knowing that this —us—is the realest thing I've ever felt.

I pull her close, her body still trembling against mine. We're a tangle of limbs, a mess of sheets barely clinging to the edge of the bed. Our skin glistens with the evidence of our desire, and every breath we take is heavy with satisfaction.

"Wow," she whispers, her voice filled with wonder and a hint of that cheeky humor I've come to adore. Her head rests on my chest, her hair a wild cascade of fire across my skin.

"Understatement of the year," I reply, my own voice hoarse with the aftermath of passion. The softness of her laughter vibrates through me, more soothing than any melody.

We're quiet for a moment, just breathing together, in and out, as if our lungs have synced up along with our heartbeats. It's intimate, this silence—more revealing than our naked bodies—and it speaks volumes about where we stand. With each heartbeat, I can feel the walls I've built around my heart crumbling, piece by piece.

"Brandon?" Erica lifts her head, those green eyes searching mine.

"Yeah?" My thumb brushes a damp strand of hair from her forehead, lingering on the softness of her skin.

"I'm yours." The words are simple, but they carry the weight of everything we've just shared.

I tighten my arms around her and plant a kiss on her forehead. "And I'm yours too, baby. Forever."

EPILOGUE

Five years later

Erica

YEARS FOLD INTO EACH OTHER, a patchwork of moments and milestones that Brandon and I have stitched together with threads of resilience and love. We dance through the trials—his deployments that stretch like endless nights, my art shows that often fall on deaf days. Yet, here we are, still us, still electric.

"Come on, babe," I coax, my voice a playful chirp as I tug on his arm. "One more round before you leave?" The military base life isn't all spit-shine and salutes. It's finding home in the heartbeat of the man who wears the uniform. And damn if I haven't made every barracks and base house our own personal canvas of love and lust.

"Erica," Brandon's blue eyes pierce mine, a flicker of that soldier's discipline in his gaze. But I know better. I see the wildfire just beneath. "You know I can't resist when you look at me like that."

"Then don't," I challenge, my free spirit unfurling between us like a flag in the wind. I've followed him across state lines and shorelines, turning temporary quarters into our forever for now. Each goodbye at the base gate is a promise whispered, each hello a world reborn.

"Every assignment, every move—I do it for us," I murmur against his lips, the taste of commitment sweet and strong between us. Because this right here, this love, it's worth every mile, every moment. And I'd trail his camo-clad shadow to the ends of the earth, just for the chance to be his peace amid the chaos.

I nip at his lips with my teeth, my pussy already growing wet.

His hands find my waist, thumbs drawing lazy circles over my hip bones. "You're incorrigible," he says, but his blue eyes are dancing with the mirth he tries so hard to hide.

"Guilty as charged," I admit, voice dropping to a sultry whisper as I lean in close, noses brushing. I can feel his breath hitch, our shared air charged with the electricity that's danced between us since the day we met.

"Remember that move you pulled last night?" I murmur, lips grazing his earlobe just so, causing a shiver to run through his frame. "Think you could do it again? Only slower this time, maybe add a twist?"

"Erica," he groans, and there's that wildfire, burning away any pretense of control. He stands abruptly, towering over me, and I'm reminded of how much I love the way he fills the space around us. He cups my face gently, thumbs tracing the high of my cheekbones, the intensity in his gaze pinning me in place.

"Twist, huh?" His voice is low, teasing,

his touch sending a bolt of heat straight through me. "You might have to demonstrate exactly what you mean."

"Wouldn't you like to know," I retort with a wicked grin, backing away just out of reach, taunting him with the promise of what's to come. It's a dance we've perfected, the push and pull, the playful battle for dominance that always ends with us tangled together, breathless and spent.

"Tease." He lunges forward, but I'm quick, darting away with a laugh that fills the room, echoing off the walls we've made our own.

"Only for you, soldier," I call back over my shoulder, throwing a look that I know will bring him to his knees. We may be surrounded by the strict order of military life, but in this space, we write our own rules—an erotic playbook of desire and devotion, each chapter more thrilling than the last.

"Come here, you little minx," Brandon growls playfully, finally capturing me in his strong arms. I let myself be caught, because there's nowhere else I'd rather be.

Here, in the circle of his embrace, I am both the wild artist and the devoted partner, painting our love in bold strokes with every whispered word, every stolen kiss.

"Caught me," I breathe out, surrendering to the moment, to him.

The air between us crackles with anticipation, each breath an unspoken promise of what's to come.

"Race you to the bedroom," I challenge, a mischievous glint in my eyes.

He smirks, the corners of his mouth turning up in a way that sends a shiver straight through me. "You're on."

We dash down the narrow hallway of our base housing, laughter mixing with the pounding of our footsteps. It's not just a race. It's a prelude to the hunger we both feel, a hunger that's become more voracious with time rather than sated by familiarity.

I reach the bedroom first, but it's a hollow victory. Brandon's right behind me, and as he slams the door shut with his boot, I'm already reaching for him. My fingers find the hem of his shirt, pulling it over his head in one fluid motion. There's an urgency to our movements, a need to be skin on skin that's palpable in every hurried tug and pull.

"Your turn," he breathes out, hands deft at the buttons of my blouse, sending them flying across the room. His touch is fire on my flesh, igniting a blaze that no distance or time apart could ever extinguish.

Garments shed like fallen leaves, we're left in the raw honesty of bare skin and burning desire. There's no hesitation, no pause as Brandon trails kisses down my neck, his hands mapping the curves he knows as well as any battlefield.

"God, Erica," he groans, and I know he feels it too—the electric connection that ties us together, the love that's as relentless and enduring as the tide.

"Brandon..." His name is a plea, a prayer, a testament to all that he is to me. And as we fall into the tangle of sheets, there's no mistaking the depth of our need, the urgency that drives us to seek out pleasure in each other's embrace.

This—this collision of hearts and bodies—is our most intimate language, and we speak it fluently, fiercely, without reservation.

Brandon's mouth descends with a hunger that sends shockwaves of desire straight to my core. "I've missed this," he murmurs against the tender skin of my inner thigh, his hot breath teasing me before his tongue finds the center of my longing.

"Ah, Brandon..." I gasp, tangling my fingers in his cropped hair as he explores me with an expertise that has my toes curling, pleasure spiraling up from the place where he lavishes his attention. The wet sounds fill the room, a testament to the lust that saturates the air between us. His name becomes a mantra on my lips, each syllable punctuated by the flick of his tongue and the gentle suckle that follows.

"You taste so damn good, baby," he growls, the vibration against my flesh sending another jolt through my system. I arch into him, lost in the sensation, in the sheer intensity of what we're sharing. This isn't just about physical gratification—it's about connection, about the silent conversations our bodies have been having since the moment we met.

"More, please, more," I plead, feeling the build of something monumental. His hands grip my hips, holding me steady as he delves deeper, his movements both a promise and a fulfillment of every whispered midnight confession we've ever traded.

It's raw and real, the way he devours me with an urgency that spells out his love more eloquently than any vow. And when I shatter, calling out his name like a sacred incantation, he curses and finally breaks, plunging his hard cock into me.

He thrusts up into me furiously, chasing his own release. At the same time, he's driving me toward another orgasm.

His eyes lock onto mine, blue flames burning with that same fierce intensity, as if to say, 'I am yours, in this and every moment.'

"Brandon!" I scream his name as another wave of pleasure crashes over me. He roars out his own release, and I feel his hot heat flooding me.

I collapse beside him, breathless and

spent, every nerve ending singing with the kind of satisfaction that only Brandon can give me. My body is still humming from the intensity of our connection, the pleasure so acute it's almost tangible, a living thing between us. I turn my head to catch his gaze, and there's a silent understanding that passes between us, a wordless acknowledgment of the profound experience we've just shared.

"Wow," I manage to exhale, the sound more of a sigh than a word. My heart is thundering, but it's not just from the physical exertion—it's full to bursting with an emotional high that makes the room seem brighter, the air sweeter.

Brandon's chest rises and falls in a rhythm that matches my own. His hand finds mine, fingers intertwining as he draws me closer. "You're incredible," he says, voice husky with emotion. The warmth in his blue eyes mirrors the heat that's still dissipating from my skin.

"Right back at you, soldier." I nuzzle into his neck, breathing in the scent of him —gunpowder and desire, a combination that's become my personal brand of aphrodisiac.

We lay there, limbs entangled, the weight of his arm around me a comforting anchor. I can feel the thud of his heartbeat against my cheek, a steady drumbeat that syncs with my own. We don't need words. Our bodies have said it all.

He tightens his hold on me, a silent vow. In the stillness of our shared living space, amidst the chaos that defines military life, we find our peace.

I trace the line of Brandon's tattoo, the one that creeps over his heart—a compass without a north, because as he once told me, I'm his true direction. His skin is warm beneath my fingertips, every ridge and muscle a familiar terrain I've explored a thousand times but can't get enough of.

"Race you to the shower," I tease, already rolling out from under the cocoon of sheets that smells like us—like sweat and spice and something undeniably us.

He chuckles, and it's that low, husky sound that always sends a thrill straight through me. "You're on, Red," he says, using the nickname that only he gets away with. Before I know it, we're tangled in a playful scuffle, half-naked and laughing as we stumble toward the bathroom.

"Cheater!" I accuse when he scoops me up and strides into the steam-filled room, his grin wicked and wide.

"Strategic advantage," he counters, kissing me hard enough to steal my breath before setting me down on the cool tiles.

The water cascades over us, hot and soothing, and our hands are everywhere at once. It's not about getting clean. It's about touching and teasing, keeping that flame between us burning bright. When he slides his fingers between my thighs, I bite back a moan, pressing into his touch.

"Brandon," I gasp, and there's a hunger in his blue eyes that tells me he's nowhere near done with me.

"Say my name again," he growls, and I do, over and over, until the sound of it becomes a mantra that rides the waves of pleasure he gives me, relentless and perfect.

Afterward, as the water turns tepid and our laughter fades to contented sighs, we wrap ourselves in towels and stroll back to the bedroom, lazy and sated. The future stretches out before us, unknown but unthreatening, because we face it together.

"Hey, Erica?" Brandon's voice pulls me from my thoughts.

"Yeah?"

"Never forget this, okay? Us, how we are right now. It's going to be one hell of a story to tell our grandkids."

"Grandkids, huh?" I smirk, tossing a pillow at him. "Getting a bit ahead of ourselves, aren't we, soldier?"

"Maybe," he admits, catching the pillow and tucking it behind his head. "But with you, I can't help thinking long term."

My heart swells, so full it might burst. We're two halves of a whole, wild and passionate and unbreakable. And as I crawl into bed beside him, pressing my body to his inked canvas, I know that this —the heat of his skin, the strength in his arms, the promise in his eyes—is where I'm meant to be.

"Long term sounds just right," I whisper, and as we drift off, wrapped up in each other, I think about all the nights yet to come. With Brandon, my soldier, every day is an adventure, every touch is a revelation, and every kiss is a vow renewed.

Want a free book from Emma Bray? Go to www.authoremmabray.com.

www.ingramcontent.com/pod-product-compliance
Lightning Source LLC
Chambersburg PA
CBHW020509160726
47991CB00007B/2873